Kidnap on the Canal

Stories linking with the History
National Curriculum Key Stage 2

First published in 1999 by Franklin Watts
96 Leonard Street, London EC2A 4XD

Text © George Buchanan 1999

Editor: Sarah Snashall
Series designer: Jason Anscomb
Consultant: Dr Anne Millard, BA Hons, Dip Ed, PhD

A CIP catalogue record for this book
is available from the British Library.

ISBN   0 7496 3352 2 (hbk)
           0 7496 3540 1 (pbk)

Dewey Classification 941.081

Printed in Great Britain

Kidnap on the Canal

Written and illustrated
by
George Buchanan

FRANKLIN WATTS
NEW YORK • LONDON • SYDNEY

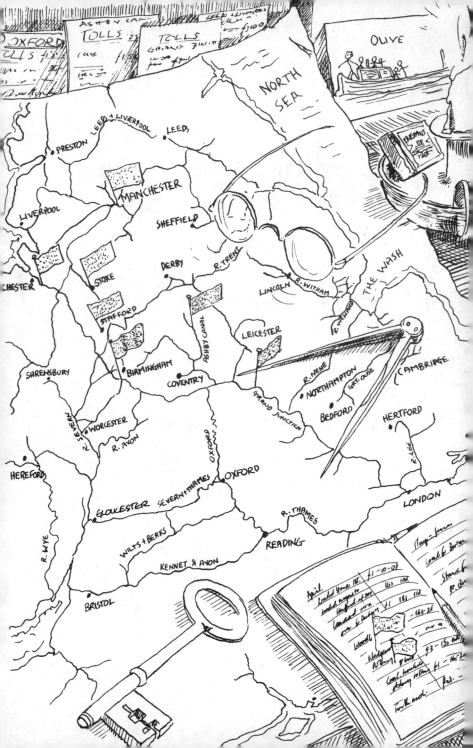

1

Noises in the Mist

The first things you notice when you wake up on our canal boat are the noises.

There's baby Rose snuffling and burbling on the floor. Buster the dog is curled up round her basket, keeping her warm. The twins, fast asleep in the top cupboard, are snoring gently. Sarah, too, is curled up, and almost pushing me off the side berth. She breathes in wheezy gasps; she must have woken me with one

of her coughs. I can hear the ducks and rats in the water, the reeds rustling and, close by, my Mum grunting and talking to herself in her sleep.

In the distance, I hear a slap-slapping of a whip beating against a cabin.

Buster does, too. He uncurls and pads to the hatchway. A boat is coming down the cut. There is a steady scrunch of cinders as a horse walks past. I hear the ripple of water as a barge glides past, and the sound of quiet, angry voices.

Someone hisses, "Jes you give me my rightful earnings, Mr Monk, or I'll…"

The barge slips past and is gone. Our boat, *Olive*, rocks in the wash, and I hear Dad stirring.

"Who was it?" I whisper, but Dad

shakes his head. In the distance we can just make out a smudge of darkness on the water. The sounds of the whip grow fainter, and all is quiet.

"Time we was getting ahead, Tom," says Dad.

He pulls on his boots and takes his short coat from the stern locker – that's the little cupboard at the back of the boat (the front of the boat we call the bows) – and we trudge along the towpath to collect our horse Charley from the stables.

★★★

It's a lovely hot afternoon and we're just rounding the last of Foxtons Bends. I'm leading Charley, and whisking flies off his head. The twins are playing on the cabin top and Baby Rose is tied to the stove pipe in case she falls. Sarah and Mum are sewing in the cabin.

We may not go more than two miles per hour, but Dad reckons we can carry bulk cargoes quicker and cheaper than any

waggoner with his strings of horses. With canals snaking into all the big towns, and rivers made navigable, we can deliver to most places. No wonder countryfolk and townies are attracted to the trade.

Up ahead I see a cluster of boats waiting by the lock gates, and a crowd is gathered peering into the chamber.

"Hold in, Dad!" I shout back.

Dad waves and steers towards the bank.

We tie up as close as we can get, and join the crowd.

A boat is wedged across the lock chamber. It's the boat that passed us this morning. Her stern is way up out of the water, the mooring rope as tight as tight. Her bows are right down, with water trickling over the deck into the hold. We can see a load of stone in the hold, and some has shifted.

"If any more stone shifts, she'll sink," mutters Dad. Two men have lowered ropes onto the bows of the boat, and are waiting for instructions.

"Captain Morris!" says one, recognising my Dad, "We needs someone small, like, to shin down an' hitch these ropes to the fore stud. Then we can hold her bows steady as we flush the lock."

"How about it, Tom?" says Dad.

2

Kidnapped

Shinning down a rope is easy! You hold tight with your hands, and grip with your feet. Then you just go hand over hand and down you go.

The boat wobbles as I land on the bows. I lean down and slip the first rope over the big iron hook at the front of the boat. A stone block slides slowly down the sloping hold. Water streams across the foredeck. The second rope is swung across and I hook it on. Water is sluicing over my feet, and pouring into the hold.

"Haul in them ropes and tie 'em to the mooring stumps!" shouts my Dad.

Men are on the top gate, opening the lock paddles. Water swirls and roars into the lock chamber. In the turbulence more stones slide towards the bows, and water cascades into the hold. The boat is trembling and swaying.

Dad has fetched a rope, and it's dangling
right above my head.

"Quick now, Tom."

I grip on tight, and fast as anything Dad hauls me up.

The narrow boat is settling in the water. Water has stopped coming over the bows, and the stern is afloat.

"She'll be all right now," says Dad.

***

"Let me meet the young hero who saved the day." A tall man leans over, and takes my hand. He presses a penny into it,

straightens up, smoothes down his
shabby blue jacket, and
looks around.

"You the father of
this fine lad?" he
asks, turning to
Dad. "I'm
Captain Monk.
I'm afraid it's my
boat that's caused
so much trouble.

"Can I borrow
your son for an
hour or two to help
me set my boat to
rights?" he asks Dad.
"Both my wretched
crew walked out on me
this morning, and
snaggled up the boat so

this would happen."

"I don't mind, Dad," I whisper. Boat people always help each other, it's our way. But what sort of crew would do that to a boat? What kind of captain was he?

"Make sure you walks back to us tonight then, Tom," says Dad. "We'll take our turn at the lock, and won't be far behind you."

★★★

Captain Monk hands me a bucket and a rope. "Can you have a go at emptying her?"

I drop the bucket into the hold, haul

it up and empty it over the side, again and again.

Two boats come through the lock. But not my parents'. *Olive* was the last to arrive, and will be the last boat to come through.

Seventy, seventy-one bucketfuls, I've nearly finished! This is hard work!

More boats emerge. What is Captain Monk doing in the cabin?

I stop bailing, creep back along the top planks, and step onto the cabin roof. I just reach the hatch when out he pops.

"Bit of a mess in there, Tom. I'm just doing a bit of tidying."

He heaves himself out, slams the door, and blinks in the sunlight.

"I shall reward you richly for this, my boy! Let's get going! There's work to be done, and stone to be delivered!"

"Do you want me to walk with the horse, Captain Monk?"

"Not necessary, Tom, Noah don't need leading. Have a swipe at the pump, would you?" he says.

I feel trapped. I would rather be on the towpath, but I clamber back into the hold, splash across to the pump, find the handle, and begin working it from side to side. Water spurts back into the canal.

"Keep pumping, Tom!" he sings out, and settles down, leaning on the cabin roof, squinting ahead into the afternoon sun.

We don't stop. Afternoon turns into evening. Mist rises from the meadows each side of the canal. At tea-time he reaches into the cabin and pulls out a huge loaf, a tub of lard and two mugs. He spreads the lard thickly over the bread, and hands it to me. There is water in the mug. "Adam's Ale," he announces, "nothing better. Cheers! We'll be stopping soon, Tom. I'll

fetch you a blanket and you can curl up on the cabin."

He leans into the cabin and pulls out a thick blanket.

"Roll up in that, and I'll call you when we stop."

But we never stop. It is almost dark when I wake. There is mist on the cut, a pale moon is rising, and not another boat in sight.

"Where are we?" I ask.

"Heading towards Derby," he says.

"But my dad is making for Oxford! It's the other way!"

"Well I never," he says. "Isn't that just bad luck."

3

On the Move

"Well, Tom! This is cosy!"

Captain Monk is crouching over the stove, stirring broth with a large spoon.

Cosy? It's disgusting!

Two candles flicker on the folding table. Their curling brown smoke snakes

up to the cabin roof and joins the smoke puffing from the open stove. The cabin is full of the gagging stink of unwashed clothes, smelly boots and coal smoke. Mum's cabin never smells bad!

Two dirty wooden bowls wait on the folding table. Captain Monk leans over and pours out the broth. Potatoes, lumps of meat, and globs of fat slither and drop into each bowl. He sits down, takes his spoon and stares around him.

I feel sick.

"Cheer up, Tom!" he says, "I clean forgot about you, honest to God! I was so busy with the horse, and the steering and all. But don't you worry, when we gets to Derby, Tom, we can put you on the  first Express Railway train to Oxford. You'll be back with your folks in no time!"

I don't believe him. He couldn't have forgotten me after all the work I'd done. And I don't believe it about the train either. Anyway, my folks won't be there, they never stop anywhere for more than a day or two. How can I possibly know where they are?

I drop my spoon, and begin to cry.

"Tom," he says "Don't cry lad, I'll see you all right, but for now we work together. You'll be my butty boy, my mate."

***

In the middle of the night, I'm woken by noises on the deck. The fire is out, and fresh air is  pouring into the cabin. Heavy feet stumble down the steps into the cabin. The doors are slammed shut and bolted.

Captain Monk
lurches past, crashes
onto the cross bed,
kicks off his boots
and falls back,
snoring heavily.

★★★

For months we
travel the canals.
We see plenty of
trains, some with
carriages, others with long
strings of trucks flying behind.

"There goes another chance!" Captain
Monk sings out when he sees one.

I pretend not to hear, and after a while
he forgets his stupid joke. But don't those
trains move fast! Captain Monk says you
can't get cheaper than water transport,

but what about speed? We might take four
days to deliver a load, but a train could do
it in one. How can you beat that?

Our cargo of building stone is
unloaded at Stoke (not Derby as he had
said), and in its place large wooden crates
of plates and cups are lowered into the hold.

We deliver them to a bustling factory
in Stafford, with its own canal, private
dockyard with steam cranes, and little
flat-bedded railway trucks drawn by ponies
to move them round the factory. Not one
breakage. The men there are impressed.

Then off we go to Moira on the Ashby

Canal for a load of coal. Two great piles are waiting at the dockside, and we load up, using two wheelbarrows and a shovel. I fill the barrows, and Captain Monk trundles them across the gangplank to empty them in the hold. It takes two days.

With 33 tons on board the decks are almost awash.

"We'll have to sheet her up, Tom," calls out Captain Monk, and we spread heavy canvas sheets over the top planks, and

lace them down over the sides. The sheets will keep the cargo dry, and stop thieves helping themselves to the coal.

It's a scary trip. Even walking along the top planks to reach the bow makes her tip and wobble until water laps over the sides.

We deliver the coal to a railway basin in Birmingham. Luckily there are dockers using mechanical grabs, and they unload the coal straight into waiting railway wagons. What a lot of smoke and dust! After we've shafted clear of the dock, using the long wooden poles we keep on the cabin roof, Captain Monk rolls up his sleeves, and helps me wash off the decks.

We have a routine. We take turns steering and cooking. Every day we leave before dawn, and it's long after dark when we haul in and tie up. Captain Monk allows me to clean the cabin, air the blankets, and scrub the bowls and pots – just like Mum would have done. The boat is much tidier and cleaner these days.

On Fridays, we stop early, stable the horse at the nearest inn, and go back together to cook. He won't let me out of sight – he thinks I'll run away. He needn't bother. I don't know these canals, I don't know where my parents are, and I have no money.

After supper, he changes into his best boots, and combs his hair. He's going out.

He leans over, points at me, and says, "Just you pass me your trousers for safe keeping now, Tom. Don't want you takin' any chances while I'm away!"

I slip under the blanket, wriggle out of the trousers and pass them up to him.

"No chances, now!" he chuckles. He bolts the doors, jumps onto the towpath, and walks away whistling. I curl up under the blankets.

I'll take my chance, Cap'n Monk, but not until we head South.

4

Winter

The wind is cold, whipping at the boat,
pushing her sideways into the bank.
Captain Monk walks ahead leading
Noah, and I steer as best I can, heaving
the massive helm against the weight of the
wind and the boat. I huddle against the

wind, wrapped in a spare blanket, with frozen feet, sore hands, and smarting eyes. Five months I've been trapped on this boat, and now it's winter.

Manchester, Liverpool, Preston Brook, past Stoke, past the Ashby Canal. Yesterday we went straight past Hawkesbury Junction. In the distance I can just see the spire of Coventry Cathedral. I know this area! We are heading South!

We are carrying bricks and stone for lock repair work on the Grand Junction. I heard the wharfinger at Preston Brook telling Captain Monk about it. He doesn't know I know. My chance is coming and

I'll be ready for it.

"Keep in the middle," yells Captain Monk.

There are great sheets of ice at the edges of the cut. I'm doing my best, but the wind is pushing the boat sideways all the time.

The trees are bare, and the fields are black and icy. Sheep huddle against the hedges. A solitary horse stands as though frozen to the ground. Heavy grey clouds creep closer. Then large, feathery snow

flakes begin to fall, blanketing out even the edges of the cut.

We haul in to the bank.

Captain Monk stomps back – his face red and chapped, his old coat spattered  with snow, and his huge red hands clenched tight in a pair of ragged socks.

"Time for a brew," he mutters, shivering, and tumbles down into the cabin. Noah sets off again. I can hear the Captain lighting the stove. The snow is getting worse; it is hard to see. I crack the whip on the cabin roof to warn other boats of our coming. Perhaps one of them will be my boat, then

I'll jump and run for it. Smack, smack, smack, smack ...

"Tea for you, butty boy," and Captain hands out a large tin mug of hot tea, "and a bucket of coal." He puts that down on the deck by my feet.

"Feed the fire. Drop 'em down the chimney. Not too much mind. Expensive, coal is."

We huddle on the deck, cradling our tea. The wind has picked up, and the snow swirls and blinds us. We open our hands against the stove pipe for warmth. Now and again I dangle a rock of coal

over the chimney and let go. We hear it rattle down the metal pipe and thud into the fire box.

"Hold in again, Tom, I'm going to walk with Noah, and see if we can get to the tunnel tonight."

Captain Monk jumps ashore, slides sideways on the snow, staggers to his feet and, hunched against the wind, marches into the blizzard.

Ice cracks and splinters against the bows as we push our way along. I can see Captain Monk stop Noah, lean over, and

scrape the snow from his hooves; then they
are off, the tow rope lifts, and flicks snow
and icicles as it snaps taut.

★★★

From ahead I can hear the cracking of a
smacking whip, and another farther away.
Two boats are approaching. I smack our
whip as a warning,
and peer into the
blinding snow.
    "Hold in there,
Tom," Captain
shouts, and before I
know it, he is back
on the deck. I can
feel his hand on my
shoulder. Nervously,
I edge to the side, ready to jump. His grip
hardens. The first horse steps past, his

hooves muffled by the snow.

The tow rope is hoisted over our stove pipe. I don't recognise the man leading the horse. A long grey barge, with a brightly

painted cabin appears out of the blizzard, and is gone.

Another barge glides by. That's the butty boat, towed by the first barge. I don't recognise her either.

Now the second horse is approaching, led by a girl younger than me. The girl whips the rope over our stove pipe, smacks the horse and is gone. I see the bows of the barge, forcing aside the sheets of ice in its way. She is empty and riding high. It's another stranger. Captain Monk taps me on the shoulder.

"Off we go, Tom," and he leaps ashore. I haul the helm towards me, and head for the clear water in the middle of the cut, sick with disappointment.

★★★

It is dark when we arrive at the entrance to the tunnel. It's stopped snowing, and the night is clear, and bitter cold.

A string of barges is waiting ahead of us. A steam tug bustles past, heading for the tunnel. It pauses and a tow rope is thrown to the first boat, then ropes are passed back from

boat to boat. Our tow line is handed to Captain Monk, who hitches it to the stud on the foredeck. He jumps ashore and walks back to me.

"Nick of time for the last tow of the day, Tom," he says happily. "You steer her through. Eleven boats ahead. We're the last. I'll walk Noah over the hill and meet you the other side. Pull in when you arrive. Don't let the fire go out. We'll want tea when you get there."

He turns, catches Noah and joins the
group of black figures heading up the hill
with their horses. Glancing back, I see
another barge just pulling into view. It is
going to miss the tow.

There is a jolt, a whistle from the tug,
and the barges pull away and snake
towards the entrance. The latecomer is
just stopping behind us. I see a tall man
with his ropes. There are children
crowding round the cabin, and a dog

jumps ashore barking …

"Dad!" I shout. But it is too late! He can't hear me. Every moment we move faster. The portal looms above me, and we slip into the smoky blackness of the tunnel.

5

Escape

My eyes adjust to the dark. The tunnel is lit by pale lamplight shining from open cabin doors. We're moving fast, faster than Noah can ever pull us.

Silently, we're drawn deeper into the dark tunnel.

The brick roof gives way to bare jagged rock. There's a distant thundering. Cabin doors are shut, hatches are pulled tight. All is blackness. I steer by feel. The noise is deafening. Suddenly, a cascade of water pours down from a ventilation shaft in the roof of the tunnel. I'm drenched and freezing.

The air is warmer as we go deeper into the hill, but it tastes of grit and coal smoke. In other boats, too, people are coughing and gasping. The tunnel seems to go on for ever.

Suddenly, in the distance, I notice a change. I can see the tug's funnel, black in a blue light, and I know we are through. We burst into the freezing air, and a bright starlit sky.

Captain Monk is waiting with Noah.

"Not stopping, Tom," he mutters, "must move on a bit."

I look at him. Could he have seen my parents' boat? Why move on at this time of night?

Without a second's delay we're off again into the dark. But now I know my parents will not be far behind

The next day we're up early. It's still

bitterly cold. Captain Monk sends me round the side decks with a pole to break

up the ice gripping our boat.

All day we head south. We pass other crews prodding and smashing the ice. We pass a short, round-fronted ice boat with men carrying coal and a brazier on its deck. We pass a cottage, and I wave to the lengthsman who is just setting off to clear the ice from the towpath. He might recognise me, and pass the word down the cut.

Today's Friday and tonight we'll stop early. And I'm ready to take my chance,

just as soon as Captain Monk has gone
to the inn.

★★★

"Well Tom, just you pass me your trousers
and I'll be off."

I squirm under the blankets and hand
out my trousers.

"Keep the fire going, Tom," he calls,
pulling on his best boots. Then he bolts
the doors and I hear his steps fade into
the distance.

I'm out of bed in
a flash. I drag out
his heavy old boots.
I open the stove and
try to force one of
them into the stove.
It's too big, so I
grab a knife.

It's quiet outside – he spends hours at the inn. Plenty of time. Needn't worry.

I take the first boot. I slit the laces, slit the stitching round the sole, separate the pieces and push

them into the stove. Then the other boot.

They burn noisily, and make a ghastly smell.

I can hear footsteps on the towpath. It's too early, Captain Monk can't be coming back already!

"Baked rhinoceros tonight is it, Captain?" someone calls, "What a stink!"

There is laughter, and then the steps die away.

I peer through the crack in the doorway.
My trousers are hanging over the helm as
usual. I crawl back to bed, and wait.

★★★

Captain Monk is coming back!

The boat lurches, he stumbles in,
smelling of smoke and beer. He sits
unsteadily on the cross bed, and kicks off
his best boots.

"Smells a bit grim in here, Tom. What
you been cooking then?"

I pretend to sleep.

He opens the stove, and a gust of
foul smoke fills the cabin.
He sniffs again and
tosses in some coal.

"You awake,
Tom?"

I open one eye

and nod sleepily.

"What's this?" he says and pulls out part of the burnt boot.

"The beef. Couldn't finish it." I murmur, and pretend to go back to sleep.

He brushes it with his sleeve, and takes a bite.

He chews for a while. "Bit tough, isn't it." He spits out something onto the floor and bends down to pick it up.

It's a small sharp nail.

"People should be more careful." Captain Monk chews quietly, then, "Yuck!"

He drops the rest on the floor, and

topples back onto the bed and begins
to snore.

Silently, I pick up one of his best boots.

I creep to the doors and push them
open. Cold air floods into the cabin, and I
hear Captain Monk stirring.

As hard as I can, I hurl the boot across
the canal, whip my trousers off the helm
and jump ashore.
Then I run for my
life down the
towpath.

"Tom! Get
back here."

I look back.
He's shaking his
fist and yelling
from the doorway.
Then he
disappears. He'll

be looking for his boots.

I hear his angry bellow, and see him bursting through the hatch and bounding onto the path. Only one boot. He's limping and hobbling. I'm always barefoot and my feet are hard, but he'll not be used to the stones or the cold.

I run for my life. On and on. I hide under a bridge and listen. I think he's given up.

I pull on my trousers, then walk along the path. My parents can't be far away.

It's biting cold. There are no boats in sight. My bare feet start to feel numb, but I walk 'til I'm too tired to go on. I curl up

under a bush, snuggle into some dry
leaves, and fall asleep.

★★★

"Look what's here!"

Two men are looking down at me.

Strong hands lift me up. Men holding
a lamp peer at me.

"Put him on the ice boat."

They lead me along the tow. Six great
horses stand steaming and stamping on
the path. The ice boat has
pulled into the bank.

I'm passed aboard.
A blanket is pulled
over my shoulders,
and someone
makes room for me
by the warm brazier.

"I don't know

where you've been," says the skipper leaning over me, "but I reckon you're Captain Morris' son. *Olive*'s the boat, isn't it?"

I sing out, "She's not far away!" and I laugh to see their faces, for they must have been watching out for me these long months past.

With a shout from the skipper, the men holding the bar begin pulling and swinging, rocking the boat to break the ice. The horses stagger forward. The tow rope snaps tight.

Ice thunders and bangs against the bows of the iron boat. With a crazy

swaying, she lurches forward.

Faster we go, and faster, heading straight for the thick ice at the edge of the canal. With a thunderous crash, the bow hits the ice and skids upwards. There's a rending crack, and we smash downwards into a sheet of spray.

Then off we go again, careering across to attack the ice on the other side. Amid the crashing and splintering of the ice, I am racing home to my family.

I laugh to myself and picture them all, asleep in the silent ice. They're in for the loudest awakening they've ever had!

The Canals

The beginnings

In 1761 the Bridgewater Canal was opened and, for the first time, barges could carry coal from the Duke of Bridgewater's coal mines at Worsley directly to Salford near Manchester. By 1765 the price of coal had fallen, sales soared and other cargoes were attracted onto this cheap and reliable form of transport.

Following its success, more canals were built, connecting towns, mines, factories and ports. At its busiest, there were over 6,000 miles (9,656 km) of navigable waterways in Britain, providing employment for nearly 100,000 boat people.

Although canal transport was cheap, it was slow. Barges could only travel at 2 mph (3.2 km/h). With the growth of the railways in the mid-19th century, and then the development of the road network in the 20th century, canals began a gradual decline. Commercial traffic ceased in the late 1960s. Canals are now used for pleasure boating.

Hard work

Boat people were skilled and hardworking. On a good day a loaded barge might travel on average

23 miles (37 km), and go through 45 locks.
Cargoes were often loaded by hand – in one day or
less, a captain and his mate would be expected to
load about 25 tons (25.4 tonnes) of cargo, or
about 14,000 bricks, with only the assistance of a
wheelbarrow, and some planks to run them aboard.

Wages were considered good, particularly for the
captain and his mate. However, most crews were
only paid when they were carrying cargo – empty
journeys were unprofitable.

Family life

With a cabin only 3m long and 2m
wide and 1.7m high, living
conditions were cramped.
Sometimes families of 6 or more
would be brought up in one cabin.
Most boatpeople were proud of their
boats and kept them immaculate,

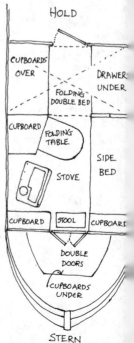

decorating the cabins with bright paintwork, polished brass and crochet ornaments.

Children would rarely go to school – their travelling life made regular attendance difficult. Instead they would learn their trade by helping their parents. Children could often steer a barge from the age of about three, standing on a stool to peer over the cabin, and many youngsters, like

Tom, would be lent by their families to help other boats that were shorthanded. By the age of fifteen, boys would be expected to leave their family and work as a mate for another skipper. By the time they were twenty, some of them would own their own boats.

Sparks: Historical Adventures

ANCIENT GREECE
The Great Horse of Troy – The Trojan War
0 7496 3369 7 (hbk)   0 7496 3538 X (pbk)
The Winner's Wreath – Ancient Greek Olympics
0 7496 3368 9 (hbk)   0 7496 3555 X (pbk)

INVADERS AND SETTLERS
Boudicca Strikes Back – The Romans in Britain
0 7496 3366 2 (hbk)   0 7496 3546 0 (pbk)
Viking Raiders – A Norse Attack
0 7496 3089 2 (hbk)   0 7496 3457 X (pbk)
Erik's New Home – A Viking Town
0 7496 3367 0 (hbk)   0 7496 3552 5 (pbk)
TALES OF THE ROWDY ROMANS
The Great Necklace Hunt
0 7496 2221 0 (hbk)   0 7496 2628 3 (pbk)
The Lost Legionary
0 7496 2222 9 (hbk)   0 7496 2629 1 (pbk)
The Guard Dog Geese
0 7496 2331 4 (hbk)   0 7496 2630 5 (pbk)
A Runaway Donkey
0 7496 2332 2 (hbk)   0 7496 2631 3 (pbk)

TUDORS AND STUARTS
Captain Drake's Orders – The Armada
0 7496 2556 2 (hbk)   0 7496 3121 X (pbk)
London's Burning – The Great Fire of London
0 7496 2557 0 (hbk)   0 7496 3122 8 (pbk)
Mystery at the Globe – Shakespeare's Theatre
0 7496 3096 5 (hbk)   0 7496 3449 9 (pbk)
Plague! – A Tudor Epidemic
0 7496 3365 4 (hbk)   0 7496 3556 8 (pbk)
Stranger in the Glen – Rob Roy
0 7496 2586 4 (hbk)   0 7496 3123 6 (pbk)
A Dream of Danger – The Massacre of Glencoe
0 7496 2587 2 (hbk)   0 7496 3124 4 (pbk)
A Queen's Promise – Mary Queen of Scots
0 7496 2589 9 (hbk)   0 7496 3125 2 (pbk)
Over the Sea to Skye – Bonnie Prince Charlie
0 7496 2588 0 (hbk)   0 7496 3126 0 (pbk)
TALES OF A TUDOR TEARAWAY
A Pig Called Henry
0 7496 2204 4 (hbk)   0 7496 2625 9 (pbk)
A Horse Called Deathblow
0 7496 2205 9 (hbk)   0 7496 2624 0 (pbk)
Dancing for Captain Drake
0 7496 2234 2 (hbk)   0 7496 2626 7 (pbk)
Birthdays are a Serious Business
0 7496 2235 0 (hbk)   0 7496 2627 5 (pbk)

VICTORIAN ERA
The Runaway Slave – The British Slave Trade
0 7496 3093 0 (hbk)   0 7496 3456 1 (pbk)
The Sewer Sleuth – Victorian Cholera
0 7496 2590 2 (hbk)   0 7496 3128 7 (pbk)
Convict! – Criminals Sent to Australia
0 7496 2591 0 (hbk)   0 7496 3129 5 (pbk)
An Indian Adventure – Victorian India
0 7496 3090 6 (hbk)   0 7496 3451 0 (pbk)
Farewell to Ireland – Emigration to America
0 7496 3094 9 (hbk)   0 7496 3448 0 (pbk)

The Great Hunger – Famine in Ireland
0 7496 3095 7 (hbk)   0 7496 3447 2 (pbk)
Fire Down the Pit – A Welsh Mining Disaster
0 7496 3091 4 (hbk)   0 7496 3450 2 (pbk)
Tunnel Rescue – The Great Western Railway
0 7496 3353 0 (hbk)   0 7496 3537 1 (pbk)
Kidnap on the Canal – Victorian Waterways
0 7496 3352 2 (hbk)   0 7496 3540 1 (pbk)
Dr. Barnardo's Boys – Victorian Charity
0 7496 3358 1 (hbk)   0 7496 3541 X (pbk)
The Iron Ship – Brunel's Great Britain
0 7496 3355 7 (hbk)   0 7496 3543 6 (pbk)
Bodies for Sale – Victorian Tomb-Robbers
0 7496 3364 6 (hbk)   0 7496 3539 8 (pbk)
Penny Post Boy – The Victorian Postal Service
0 7496 3362 X (hbk)   0 7496 3544 4 (pbk)
The Canal Diggers – The Manchester Ship Canal
0 7496 3356 5 (hbk)   0 7496 3545 2 (pbk)
The Tay Bridge Tragedy – A Victorian Disaster
0 7496 3354 9 (hbk)   0 7496 3547 9 (pbk)
Stop, Thief! – The Victorian Police
0 7496 3359 X (hbk)   0 7496 3548 7 (pbk)
Miss Buss and Miss Beale – Victorian Schools
0 7496 3360 3 (hbk)   0 7496 3549 5 (pbk)
Chimney Charlie – Victorian Chimney Sweeps
0 7496 3351 4 (hbk)   0 7496 3551 7 (pbk)
Down the Drain – Victorian Sewers
0 7496 3357 3 (hbk)   0 7496 3550 9 (pbk)
The Ideal Home – A Victorian New Town
0 7496 3361 1 (hbk)   0 7496 3553 3 (pbk)
Stage Struck – Victorian Music Hall
0 7496 3367 0 (hbk)   0 7496 3554 1 (pbk)
TRAVELS OF A YOUNG VICTORIAN
The Golden Key
0 7496 2360 8 (hbk)   0 7496 2632 1 (pbk)
Poppy's Big Push
0 7496 2361 6 (hbk)   0 7496 2633 X (pbk)
Poppy's Secret
0 7496 2374 8 (hbk)   0 7496 2634 8 (pbk)
The Lost Treasure
0 7496 2375 6 (hbk)   0 7496 2635 6 (pbk)

20th-CENTURY HISTORY
Fight for the Vote – The Suffragettes
0 7496 3092 2 (hbk)   0 7496 3452 9 (pbk)
The Road to London – The Jarrow March
0 7496 2609 7 (hbk)   0 7496 3132 5 (pbk)
The Sandbag Secret – The Blitz
0 7496 2608 9 (hbk)   0 7496 3133 3 (pbk)
Sid's War – Evacuation
0 7496 3209 7 (hbk)   0 7496 3445 6 (pbk)
D-Day! – Wartime Adventure
0 7496 3208 9 (hbk)   0 7496 3446 4 (pbk)
The Prisoner – A Prisoner of War
0 7496 3212 7 (hbk)   0 7496 3455 3 (pbk)
Escape from Germany – Wartime Refugees
0 7496 3211 9 (hbk)   0 7496 3454 5 (pbk)
Flying Bombs – Wartime Bomb Disposal
0 7496 3210 0 (hbk)   0 7496 3453 7 (pbk)
12,000 Miles From Home – Sent to Australia
0 7496 3370 0 (hbk)   0 7496 3542 8 (pbk)